Sports Illustrated KIDS

STARS OF SPORTS

AARON JUDGE

HOME RUN HERO

■ ■ by Ryan G. *Van* Cleave

CAPSTONE PRESS
a capstone imprint

Published by Capstone Press, an imprint of Capstone
1710 Roe Crest Drive, North Mankato, Minnesota 56003
capstonepub.com

Library of Congress Cataloging-in-Publication Data
Names: Van Cleave, Ryan G., 1972- author.
Title: Aaron Judge : home run hero / by Ryan G. Van Cleave.
Description: North Mankato, MN : Capstone Press, [2025] | Series: Sports illustrated kids stars of sports | Audience: Ages 8-11 | Audience: Grades 4-6 | Summary: "Aaron Judge was a big kid with big talent. He was a star in basketball, baseball, and football. Many colleges tried to recruit him to play football, but his true love was always baseball. From smashing a home run in his first at-bat with the Yankees to winning the Home Run Derby his rookie year, Judge was made for big moments. Find out all about this superstar slugger in this captivating sports biography"— Provided by publisher. Identifiers: LCCN 2023039294 (print) | LCCN 2023039295 (ebook) | ISBN 9781669076506 (hardcover) ISBN 9781669076544 (paperback) | ISBN 9781669076551 (pdf) | ISBN 9781669076568 (epub) | ISBN 9781669076575 (kindle edition) Subjects: LCSH: Judge, Aaron, 1992—Juvenile literature. | Baseball players—United States— Biography—Juvenile literature. Classification: LCC GV865.J83 V36 2025 (print) | LCC GV865.J83 (ebook) DDC 796.357092 [B]—dc23/eng/20230925
LC record available at https://lccn.loc.gov/2023039294
LC ebook record available at https://lccn.loc.gov/2023039295

Editorial Credits
Editor: Christianne Jones; Designer: Jaime Willems; Media Researcher: Svetlana Zhurkin; Production Specialist: Whitney Schaefer

Image Credits
Associated Press: Eric Francis, 10, Kathy Willens, 24; Getty Images: Dustin Satloff, 7, Elsa, 25, Michelle Farsi, 27, Mike Ehrmann, 5, Mike Stobe, 18, New York Yankees, 9, Rich Schultz, 17, Ron Jenkins, 20, Sarah Stier, cover, 21, 28, WireImage/ Cassidy Sparrow, 23; Newscom: Cal Sport Media/Josh Holmberg, 13, Cal Sport Media/Peter Joneleit, 19, Icon SMI/Rich Graessle, 14, Icon Sportswire/Cliff Welch, 15; Shutterstock: Eugene Onischenko, 1, Jim Feliciano, 12

Source Notes
Page 6, "I didn't like it as . . ." David Fischer, *Aaron Judge: The Incredible Story of the New York Yankees' Home Run-Hitting Phenom.* Sports Publishing, 2022, page 13.

Page 8, "I know I wouldn't . . ." "6 things you need to know about Yankees star Aaron Judge," *USA Today,* July 3, 2017, https://www.usatoday.com/story/sports/mlb/yankees/2017/07/03/6-things-you-need-know-yankees-star-aaron-judge/447500001, Accessed May 2023.

Page 12, "I just didn't think . . ." "Here's how the Yanks landed Judge in '13 Draft," MLB, October 4, 2022, https://www.mlb.com/ yankees/news/featured/oral-history-of-yankees-drafting-aaron-judge-c278026828, Accessed June 2023.

Page 16, "I come to the park . . ." David Fischer, *Aaron Judge: The Incredible Story of the New York Yankees' Home Run-Hitting Phenom.* Sports Publishing, 2022, page 39.

Page 21, "I'm just trying to be the best . . ." "Yankees' Aaron Judge joins Babe Ruth, Mickey Mantle in special club," NJ.com, June 5, 2022, https://www.msn.com/en-us/sports/mlb/yankees-aaron-judge-joins-babe-ruth-mickey-mantle-in-special-club-its-an-honor/ar-AAY6viI, Accessed May 2023.

Page 21, "I never want . . ." "Aaron Judge, in Yankees Camp Early, Discusses His Recovering Shoulder," *New York Times,* February 14, 2018, https://www.nytimes.com/2018/02/14/sports/yankees-aaron-judge.html, Accessed May 2023.

Page 25, "The kid seems . . ." David Fischer, *Aaron Judge: The Incredible Story of the New York Yankees' Home Run-Hitting Phenom.* Sports Publishing, 2022, page 116.

Page 28, "One of my dreams . . ." David Fischer, *Aaron Judge: The Incredible Story of the New York Yankees' Home Run-Hitting Phenom.* Sports Publishing, 2022, page 36.

Printed and bound in the USA. PO 5853

TABLE OF CONTENTS

Words in **BOLD** are in the glossary.

SWINGING FOR THE FENCES

Aaron Judge took a deep breath. He adjusted his batting gloves. He needed just one more home run to win the 2017 Home Run Derby. This competition is part of Major League Baseball's (MLB) annual All-Star Game. The only two players left were Judge and Minnesota Twins star Miguel Sanó. Sanó had smashed 10 homers in the final round. Judge now had 10, and the clock was ticking.

The crowd was on his side. Judge won them over with his strength, skill, and power. The balls shot like rockets off his bat.

The pitch came fast. Judge swung hard. THWACK! The ball shot up, up, up. The crowd cheered. For the first time, a **rookie** won Major League Baseball's Home Run Derby.

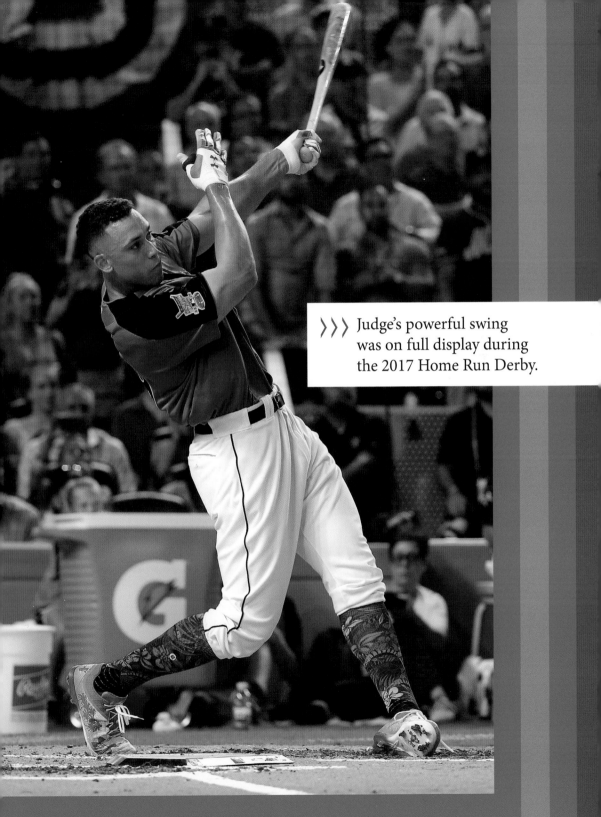

>>> Judge's powerful swing was on full display during the 2017 Home Run Derby.

CHAPTER ONE

DREAMING BIG FROM THE START

Aaron James Judge was born April 26, 1992, in the small town of Linden, California. He grew up with loving parents, Patty and Wayne Judge. He had one older brother, John.

Judge's parents were both teachers. They made education a priority. No video games or playtime was allowed until homework and chores were done.

"I didn't like it as a kid," Judge says, "but looking back on it, I really appreciated what they did for me."

>>> Judge poses with his dad, wife (second from left), and his mom at a press conference in 2022.

Judge always knew he didn't look like his white parents. One day, he asked them about it. They explained that Judge and his brother were adopted. He said, "Okay. Can I go outside and play?"

Throughout his childhood, Judge was bigger and stronger than other kids. By age 10, he was taller than his teachers! And in T-ball, he hit the ball so hard that opponents turned away or moved to protect themselves.

Family Is Everything

Judge calls his parents every day. "I know I wouldn't be a New York Yankee if it wasn't for my mom," Judge said. "The guidance she gave me as a kid growing up, knowing the difference from right and wrong, how to treat people and how to go the extra mile and put in extra work, all that kind of stuff. She's molded me into the person that I am today."

>>> Judge talks with his mom after setting a record during a game in 2022.

In high school, Judge became a three-sport star. He was a pitcher and first baseman in baseball, a center in basketball, and a wide receiver in football. In his senior year at Linden High School, Judge set the school touchdown record with 17. He led the basketball team in points per game at 18.2.

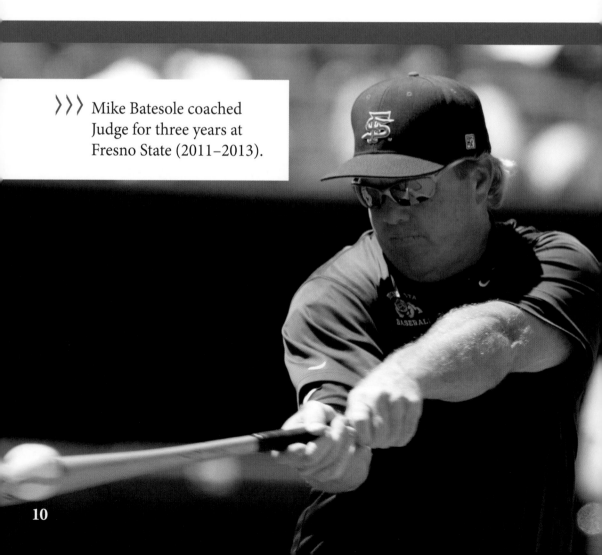

⟩⟩⟩ Mike Batesole coached Judge for three years at Fresno State (2011–2013).

Top college teams such as Stanford, Notre Dame, and UCLA **recruited** him for football. But Judge's heart belonged to baseball. He wanted to stay on the West Coast so he could be near his family. The college his parents attended, Fresno State, was only two hours away. And its baseball coach had a reputation for creating great players who were very good citizens. It was a perfect fit.

FACT

In high school, Judge did a lot of community service. His favorite way to help was picking up trash with his basketball teammates.

CHAPTER TWO

OVERCOMING OBSTACLES

The Oakland Athletics **drafted** Judge in the 31st round of the 2010 MLB draft. But he chose to attend Fresno State University instead. "I just didn't think I was ready or mature enough mentally or physically to start pro ball," he said.

>>> Campus of Fresno State University, California

While Judge was a star high school athlete, he faced challenges with college baseball. At this level, being big wasn't enough. He had to learn how to hit against tough pitchers. He had to improve his fielding skills. Judge worked hard, learning valuable lessons about perseverance and dedication.

FACT

At 282 pounds (128 kilograms) and 6 feet, 7 inches (201 centimeters) tall, Judge is the biggest position player in MLB history.

〉〉〉 Judge hits a single during a college game in 2013.

>>> Judge in a New York Yankees jersey at the 2013 draft

After three years of being a first-team all-conference college baseball player, Judge's dream came true. In 2013, the New York Yankees selected him with the 32nd overall pick in the draft. But he tore a thigh muscle during a base-running **drill**. The injury kept him out of the entire 2013 season.

FACT

When Judge signed a contract with the Yankees in 2013, he received a $1.8 million signing **bonus**.

>>> Judge bats during a minor-league spring training game.

Like most drafted players, Judge had to first prove himself in Minor League Baseball. He spent several seasons with the Charleston RiverDogs, Trenton Thunder, and other minor-league teams. He did well, but a knee sprain put him on the injured list for an entire month in 2016. He was *so* close to reaching his dream!

Judge's hard work paid off when the Yankees called him up at last. He made his major-league **debut** August 13, 2016. In his first at-bat, he smashed a home run. But a chest injury ended his season early with a disappointing .179 batting average. At Fresno State, he had an impressive .345 average.

"I come to the park every day with the goal of being better than I was the day before," Judge said. "I feel that if I can do that each day, I will get to where I want to be."

>>> Judge sends the ball sailing for a home run in his first MLB at-bat.

CHAPTER THREE

STAR SLUGGER

Judge's success with the New York Yankees was nothing short of amazing. He quickly became known as a **slugger**. He broke the rookie home run record with 52 homers.

On September 30, 2017, Judge hit a jaw-dropping 496-foot (152-meter) home run. It was the longest of the MLB season. It helped him earn the title of American League (AL) Rookie of the Year. In 2022, he hit 60 home runs earlier in the season than any other player in AL history.

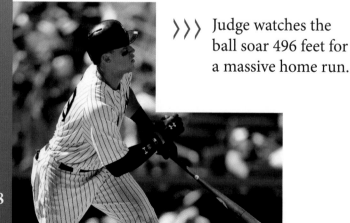

〉〉〉 Judge watches the ball soar 496 feet for a massive home run.

Lucky Bubble Gum

Judge has a bubble gum superstition. During games, he always chomps on two pieces of Dubble Bubble. If he gets a hit, he sticks with the same gum. If he doesn't, he swaps in new gum.

One of Judge's most memorable moments came on October 4, 2022. He hit his record-breaking 62nd home run for a season. This shattered Roger Maris's single-season AL home run record from 1961. Judge's home run ball sold for $1.5 million at **auction**!

FACT

The right field of Yankee Stadium features a section of seats called "The Judge's Chambers." The section looks like a courtroom jury box.

〉〉〉 Estevan Florial (right) celebrates with Judge.

Fans everywhere admire Judge's skill and power. But they also appreciate his sportsmanship, teamwork, and love for his community. Even with all the fame and attention, Judge remains respectful and **humble**. "I'm just trying to be the best Aaron Judge I can be," he said, "and I just want to stay consistent for this team and keep this thing rolling."

Judge is known for encouraging his teammates. He's always ready with a high-five to celebrate their achievements. Judge plays with heart, giving his all in every game. "I never want to play timid or scared of anything," he explained, "especially when my pitcher or my teammates are out there going 100 percent."

CHAPTER FOUR

MAKING A DIFFERENCE

Judge's commitment to being a good teammate and making a difference in the community is inspiring. From the beginning of his MLB career, he wanted to give back and inspire others. He's involved in many charitable activities. These include working with the Make-A-Wish Foundation and the Boys and Girls Club.

Judge took his passion for helping others even further by creating the ALL RISE Foundation. This organization engages children in activities that encourage them to reach higher. It looks to inspire children to become responsible citizens.

FACT

In 2023, Judge won the Roberto Clemente Award. This honor is given to a player who exhibits exceptional sportsmanship and actively contributes to his community.

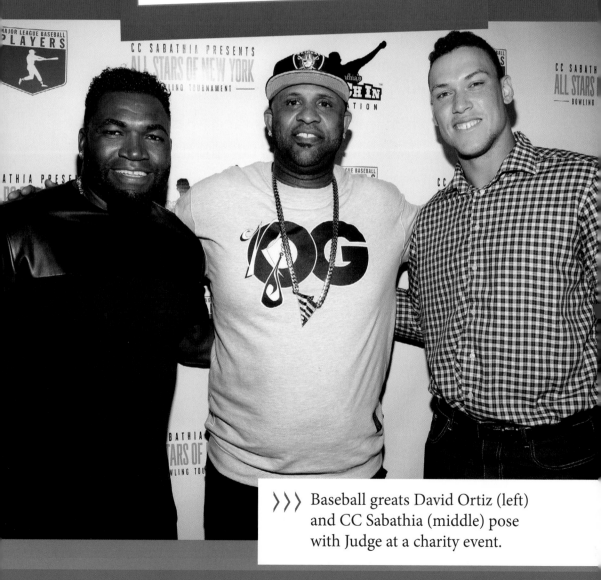

〉〉〉 Baseball greats David Ortiz (left) and CC Sabathia (middle) pose with Judge at a charity event.

Every year, the Yankees have HOPE Week. The team uses its platform to shine a light on local heroes and organizations every day for a week. Judge is an **ambassador** for the team. Attention from celebrities like Judge can help raise awareness that can forever change a group or cause.

In 2022, Landis Sims was one of the HOPE honorees. Sims was born without hands or feet. That did not stop him from making his varsity baseball team. Judge got to meet Sims and talk about baseball before he threw out the first pitch at a game.

〉〉〉 Landis Sims, a New York Yankees fan, throws out the first pitch before a baseball game in 2017.

>>> Yankee teammates Matt Carpenter (left) and Aaron Hicks (middle) cheer from the dugout with Judge.

Like so many, Yankees radio broadcaster John Flaherty admires Judge. "The kid seems to have his head on his shoulders the right way. He seems to say the right thing. It's about team first, it's not about him."

CHAPTER FIVE

WHAT'S NEXT?

Aaron Judge has achieved so much in his baseball career. But he's not stopping anytime soon! He has already earned a mountain of awards. He's a five-time All-Star, an AL Most Valuable Player (MVP), and a two-time All-MLB first-team member.

Baseball experts and fans alike are excited to see what Judge will accomplish next. His incredible talent has many people believing that he will continue to make history in the sport.

MLB World Champion Brett Gardner said, "He's worth the price of admission just to come see him play in person for nine innings." Aaron Boone is a former MLB player and current manager of the New York Yankees. Boone said, "I think he's a great face of the game, a representative of the game."

New York
Chapter

New Y
Chap

>>> Judge holds his 2022
American League MVP
plaque and two other
important awards.

So, what's next for Judge? Will he break more records, win more awards, or lead the Yankees to a World Series championship? One thing's for sure. He's going to be a Yankee for a long, long time. He signed a nine-year, $360 million contract in 2022.

Judge said, "One of my dreams is to be one of the next great ones, but I know I have to work hard every day to work toward that goal."

>>> Judge sends a ball out of the park against the Tampa Bay Rays in 2023.

TIMELINE

1992 — Born April 26 in Linden, California

2007 — Becomes star player of his high school baseball team

2010 — Graduates from high school and starts college at Fresno State University

2011 — Named the Western Athletic Conference Freshman of the Year and earns All-WAC First Team honors

2013 — Drafted by the New York Yankees in the first round (32nd overall).

2014 — Hits 17 home runs in his first full minor-league season

2016 — Hits a home run during his first at-bat as a Yankee

2017 — Selected as a starter for the All-Star Game for the first time

2017 — Wins Home Run Derby at the MLB All-Star Game

2017 — Hits a 496-foot home run—the longest of his career

2017 — Breaks rookie record for home runs in a season

2017 — Wins the Silver Slugger Award for the first time (also wins it in 2021 and 2022)

2018 — Launches the ALL RISE Foundation

2022 — Signs a nine-year, $360 million contract with the Yankees

GLOSSARY

AMBASSADOR (am-BA-suh-duhr)—a person picked to represent a group

AUCTION (AWK-shun)—a sale where goods are sold to the person who bids the most money

BONUS (BOH-nus)—extra money a worker receives

DEBUT (DAY-byu)—someone's first appearance or performance

DRAFT (DRAFT)—the process of selecting new players to join a professional sports team

DRILL (DRIL)—to practice something over and over

HUMBLE (HUHM-bul)—not bragging about your abilities or achievements

RECRUIT (ri-KROOT)—to ask someone to join a team

ROOKIE (RUH-kee)—a first-year player

SLUGGER (SLUG-uhr)—a power hitter who often hits home runs

READ MORE

Buckley, James Jr. *Who Is Aaron Judge?* New York: Penguin Workshop, 2024.

Hewson, Anthony K. *Aaron Judge.* Minnetonka, MN: Kaleidoscope, 2019.

Martin, Andrew. *Baseball's Greatest Players: 10 Baseball Biographies for New Readers.* Emeryville, CA: Rockridge Press, 2022.

INTERNET SITES

Aaron Judge ALL RISE Foundation
aaronjudgeallrisefoundation.org

Major League Baseball
mlb.com

New York Yankees
yankees.com

INDEX

AUTHOR BIO

Ryan G. Van Cleave is the author of dozens of books for children and hundreds of articles published in magazines. As The Picture Book Whisperer, they help celebrities write books for children. Ryan lives in Florida.